# Sharing the Mou

## The First Year

Table of Contents

# Introduction

There are things in this world that we cannot fully understand or just unwilling to accept.

I have never told anyone outside of my family what I am going to tell you in this book. It's something that's so taboo that I was afraid that people would laugh at me or think I was crazy. But it's true to my best recollection of the weird and sometimes unbelievable experiences that my family went through living in the woods of the Appalachian Mountains.

My husband, Jake's dream, was to have a farm and lots of lands to call his own. We were married in 1975, and right away we started looking for some land or farm to purchase. In the meantime, we lived in a little house that we rented in a town where we both worked. We were saving money for our first big purchase when I became pregnant with our first child Cody Lynn who was born on December 2, 1976.

Being a mother for the first time was very overwhelming at first but very rewarding. I left my job just to stay at home with our beautiful child while Jake worked all the hours he could at his job. We were still saving money for our farm, but it was taking longer to save up more money. On June 28, 1978, we welcomed our second child to our family and she was named Emma Grace.

Jake kept working long hours, and we saved what we thought would be a very good down payment on some property, and we were very anxious to find our dream home. We were tired of the city life and wanted to raise our children where they could run and play in the yard and learn how to grow their own food and take care of animals. We also wanted to have a farm where Jake could quit his job in the city and produce enough income from our farm.

One beautiful Saturday afternoon, we jumped into the car and took off heading to the mountains. We came up to a driveway, and we stopped. Right beside the driveway was a sign that said, "Farm for Sale." We couldn't believe our luck! We pulled into the driveway and noticed that the road was in a very bad shape. Trees were overgrown on both sides, and pot holes were abundant. We slowly drove up the driveway and finally came to an opening, and that was when we saw the old house that looked to be abandoned.

We got out of the car and just stared at the old two-story farmhouse with a big front porch. It was in a neglected shape, but in my heart, I knew we could fix it up and make it beautiful. Next, we walked around the side of the house and noticed a big barn. Perfect! It was big enough for lots of farm animals. Also, about at least three acres of land was cleared around the house. Dense woods surrounded the three acres.

We knew that the owners were not there, so we drove back down the driveway and jotted the phone number down.

I tried to contact the owners as soon as we got to our house in town. A couple of weeks later the owner contacted us back. We couldn't believe the price she wanted for the farm. We could almost pay cash for the property, not just a big down payment. We couldn't believe it. We were just surprised. She also said we would have to take it "as is" because she was unable and refused to meet us there to look at the property. She also told us that the property was eight acres with a gently flowing river running through it on the back side of the property line.

We went back to the farm to see what will require maintenance. The house and barn were not in bad shape, surprisingly, all except for the barn that had one of the double doors destroyed. It was laying on the ground in front of the barn. No big deal. We can buy another barn door. The house did need new windows and doors, but the old ones were not broken, and that can wait until we have moved in. We fell in love with this farm, and we purchased the property.

# CHAPTER 1

## Spring 1979

Moving to our farm was very exciting, and we all were in happy moods. Even our one-year-old Emma could sense the excitement in the air. The big farmhouse was beautiful. Stepping inside the front door was a huge living room with a very big fireplace. The room needed painting, but that would have to wait. Also, in the living room to the left, there was a big beautiful staircase leading up to the second level of the house to the bedrooms. Next to the front living room, going to the back of the house, was the kitchen. It was also a spacious room with a closet on the far side of the wall to the right and cabinets going around where the stove and oven were located on the left side of the kitchen. The back wall where the sink had big beautiful windows and a back door. Those were the only two rooms on the first level of the house. The bedrooms were on the second floor with three generous size rooms and a master bedroom at the back of the house. As you walk up the staircase in front of the house and walk down the hallway, there was a bedroom on the left and one on the right, with the bathroom right next to the bedroom to the left. The master bedroom was at the end of the hallway and took up the rest of the upstairs, which had big windows looking out in the backyard. We didn't have much to move, and our modest furniture didn't fill up to half of the farm house. But we didn't care. We would need plenty of time to buy stuff for our new home.

After a couple of days, we were settled in and enjoying our new home. It was Saturday, and Jake was getting ready to go to town to buy a new door for the barn. The morning was a bit chilly, but with it being a sunny day, it was warming up outside, and I wanted to get some fresh air in the house. I started opening all the windows in the house. When I got to the kitchen windows at the back of the house, looking out to the back yard with a covered back porch, I thought of how nice it would be to go for a walk and enjoy the sunshine. I could see the small path from the window in the kitchen going into the woods behind the house.

I took Cody and Emma, helped Cody with his coat, wrapped Emma in a blanket, picked her up, and went out through the back door in the kitchen, onto the covered porch, and started heading to the tree line to the path while Cody started running in front.

We started walking on the path, and I notice that the path is much worn.

"I wonder who's been walking on this path," I said to myself. No one has been living in the house for a long time now, but the path behind the house has frequently been used.

"Maybe hunters?" I said aloud.

We continued walking down the path for some time, and we started hearing water running. I catch up to Cody, and we came out of the woods to a beautiful site. We found a gently flowing river! The river was about thirty feet across and not very deep. Maybe in the middle was deep but I couldn't tell how deep.

The path that we were on went straight into the river. I looked to the right where the tall grass was and saw another small path leading to a sandy part by the river where a huge boulder sat. I grabbed Cody's hand, with Emma on my hip, and followed the small path to the boulder. It was a little part of a paradise! A sandy little beach with a boulder to sit on right beside the river.

"We will visit this place often in the summer," I told the children. Cody loved the place.

Suddenly, I noticed something wasn't quite right. When we were walking on the path, we heard the birds singing and the squirrels rustling around. Now everywhere was quiet, except for the flowing river. I didn't think much about it, and we started throwing rocks into the river. Cody was having a fun time, and I was giving Emma a pebble to throw in the river when out of nowhere Cody said "hi" and started waving at someone or something across the river.

I looked up to see who he was waving to but didn't see anyone. "Who are you waving to Cody?" I asked.

"Big man over there," he said and pointed to the other side of the river.

I looked to where he was pointing, but no one was there. That's when the most putrid smell I have ever smelled came over us. Three-year-old Cody came running to me holding his nose and saying,

"Smell bad, smell bad," still pointing to the other side of the river.

I picked Emma up and took Cody's hand and said to them "it's time to go back to the house, daddy will be back soon and we have to help him with the barn door."

With that said, Cody was ready to leave the river.

We started heading back to the house on the well-beaten path when I heard something walking behind us. That startled me. I picked up Cody with my free hand and start walking faster. I knew there are bears and mountain lions in the Appalachian Mountains and I did not want to run into either one.

My heart started to pound, and I am almost going into a jog. The path seems like it is getting longer and longer and I thought I must have taken the wrong path, even though I saw only one path when we came out. I began to panic; my breathing became heavier and faster, and I could hear my heart beating in my ears. I started running as fast as I could with my two children in my arms. But finally, I saw the opening of the woods, just in time to see Jake coming up the driveway. What a relief that was!

I was close to the side of the house before I put Cody down and he ran up to his dad. I stopped walking and turned around to see what was behind me all this while. I didn't see anything following us. And the birds were singing again. I thought that my imagination was running wild.

I walked up to Jake and gave him a gentle kiss on the cheek. He took Emma, gave her a kiss, and he looked at me and said "what have you all been up to? You look a little pale. Are you feeling okay?"

By that time, I had calmed down a little and was breathing calmly again, and my heart rate was going back to normal. I told him that we found a path that leads to the river and I had to carry both children and I was just a little winded. I didn't tell him anything else. By then, I thought it wasn't that important.

I went inside the house to attend to the children and started preparing lunch while Jake puts the barn door up. I put the children down for a nap and started closing all the windows in the house. I got to the master bedroom windows on the second floor that faces the back yard when I noticed something was moving in the woods, right beside the path. I couldn't decide out what it was because it was hidden from my view by the thick brush and trees. I kept staring out of the window, but I couldn't see it anymore, and I closed the window. I came downstairs and went to the kitchen and started closing the windows. I kept looking out to the path to see if I could see anything and when Jake came into the kitchen and startled me, I jumped and shrieked.

"What's wrong with you?" he asked.

"Nothing," I said. "I got a little spooked when we went to the river. It felt like someone was following us up the path, but you know it was probably squirrels rustling in the leaves."

"I don't think it's a good idea for you and the kids to be walking in those woods when I'm not here," Jake said.

"Okay," I said as I put a frying pan on the stovetop, not wanting to argue with him.

After lunch, Jake was heading back down the driveway to purchase our first farm animals. While he was gone, I went outside to sit in my rocking chair on the back porch watching the children play in the backyard.

Emma enjoyed playing in the sandbox, and Cody thought he was helping daddy mow the lawn with his toy lawn mower. I sat there watching the children play, but I have a feeling of being watched. I kept looking around, especially in the woods where the path was and the surrounding area.

Why do I feel this way? I kept asking myself. "I'm just silly I thought, there's nothing here, and I'm just used to the city." But I still couldn't shake the feeling of being watched.

I held the children and took them inside the house. It wasn't long before I heard Jake coming up the driveway with our new farm animals. He has built a pen for hogs on the far side of the barn, so we all knew he was going to bring the first hogs home.

We all were outside watching Jake put the hogs in the pen when we start smelling an awful smell. The same smell as we encountered at the river earlier. Jake was busy with the hogs when he stopped what he was doing and stared into the woods. He had a strange look on his face but didn't say anything. He finished putting the hogs in and made sure they had food and water, and we went back into the house. It was getting late, and dinner was overdue.

After dinner, the children needed to have their bath, and after that, I got them ready for bed. I took Emma to her bed and went downstairs to the front living room where Jake was relaxing in his rocker. I asked him if hogs have that bad of a strong smell as we smelled earlier.

"No," he said. "I don't think I have ever smelled that before. But we are in the country now, so there are different smells we will encounter than in the city."

That's all I needed to hear. I relaxed, picked my book up and thumbed through the pages where I left off. It didn't take long before I fell asleep.

A few weeks later, we were settled in our little paradise. We were getting used to all the different sounds of country living. I wasn't as jumpy as I was at first when hearing strange noises and the children absolutely loved playing in the yard.

The weather has been changing, and with that, we have had many thunderstorms. But when it's not raining, the days are warm and beautiful. While Jake is at work in the city, the children and I, after my chores, enjoyed going outside and exploring the property. We walked down the long driveway, played in the front yard as well as the back yard. We also checked on the hogs to make sure they are doing okay. Jake had also purchased chickens, and we went to see if we have any eggs yet.

About every day when we go outside and get closer to the back woods, we smell that same pungent odor as we have before. The smell is very musky with a skunk odor. It is so strong and very powerful that it will make anyone's stomach turn and ready to vomit. Cody, when he smells the odor, he will run to me covering his nose with his hand. When we smell the odor, we all will go into the house for a while.

One day Cody, Emma and I were walking down the driveway to check the mailbox to see if we have any mail. Cody's favorite thing is to look in the mailbox for letters. He thought that people were writing him letters and he was very excited to find any mail in the mailbox. The pot holes in the driveway have been filled in, and the trees on both sides are very old mature trees. It looks as if we were going in a tunnel when we went down the driveway because the limbs of the tree on each side touches at the top making the tunnel. There are also very thick woods on both sides of the drive. No one has ever cut these woods.

We walked to the mailbox at the end of the drive and started going back to the house when suddenly noticed that the woods were very quiet. No birds were making sounds. That's when I heard two knocks on a tree that came from the right side of me. Then, I heard two knocks on the left side of me. It wasn't too far away from where we were. I then heard a "whoop" sound that was very close to us and very loud.

I picked up Emma and grabbed Cody's hand, and we started walking faster. I have never heard of any animal that makes a whoop sound like the one I heard that day. Cody kept looking at me with wide eyes and a worried look on his face and asked me "what's that noise mommy," and I told him it was just a bird. Cody being only three years old, that seemed to satisfy him, and he didn't seem to be all that scared after that. But I was getting scared myself.

We made it back to the house, and we went in to have lunch. After lunch, I made the children have a nap, and I went out to hang laundry on the line to dry. I went to the clothes line and put my basket of clothes down on the ground. That was when I saw something that was not normal.

A footprint! Not just any footprint, but a huge footprint. It had been raining a lot the past few days, and there were still muddy places in the yard. And right on the clothes line, there was a muddy spot. That's where I found the footprint. I knew that none of us or even Jake has been out of the house without shoes on. So, I knew it wasn't any of our prints. Not only that, but this print was huge! I looked at it and studied it for a good while and noticed it had five toes and it had to be very heavy for the print to be deep in the mud.

I hurried and hung the clothes on the line and went inside the house. When Jake came home from work that evening, I told him about it. He went out to look at it, and came in and told me he doesn't know what kind of animal that could make that kind of print. He also looked very concerned. He went outside to feed the animals, came back in and still looked concerned.

"Tomorrow we are going to get a dog," Jake said.

"Okay" I replied, "what kind of dog?"

"A big dog. A dog that will protect the animals and the place around here. One that will run off bigger animals."

The next day was Saturday, and we loaded the children in the truck and headed down the road to our neighbor's house. John and Karen lived about a mile from our house and were very good people. They were in their early fifties and had been living at their place for many years. They raised their three children there and now that their children have moved out, it's just the two of them now. They also had a farm with farm animals and planted wheat on acres of land. They had about five big German shepherd dogs running around their property.

We visited our neighbors for a while and had lunch with them. When it was time for us to leave, John asked Jake if we had any dogs or any kind of protection for ourselves and our animals. We said no, and John's weary look on his face was very noticeable.

"You really need some kind of protection at your place," John said. "There are bears and mountain lions around here and other big animals too."

"We are going to get a dog today. But, what do you mean by other big animals? What other big animals are you talking about?" asked Jake.

John looks at Karen, while Jake and I looked at John, then back to Karen waiting for him to answer.

"Take one of these German shepherds, it will protect your livestock, and he is good with children too," John said as he looked at two dogs that were standing behind him.

He pointed to one, "Take this one, he's an obedient dog. His name is Atlas.

"I don't want to take your dog away from you," Jake said.

"You will need him," John said as he lowered the tailgate of our truck and Atlas jumped into the truck.

We thanked John and Karen for dinner and the dog as we were getting into the truck. We said our goodbye's and drove down the driveway and went back to our house.

As we drove back to our farm, the feeling of terror crept over me as I think back on our conversation with John and Karen. What do they mean by "other big animals in our woods?" What do they know that we don't? I asked myself.

A few weekends later, Jake, Cody, Emma, Atlas, and I were heading down the path to the river to go fishing. The river was swollen from all the rain we had in the past week. It was still a beautiful place. I took Emma to the little sandy beach where the boulder sits, while Jake helped Cody with his fishing pole on the other side of the main path. From where I was sitting with Emma, I could see Jake and Cody very well. Jake started fishing and was in his own world when suddenly, Cody started to wave at someone or something from across the river again. I turned as quickly as I could to see who he is waving at. Again, I didn't see anyone. I looked at Atlas as he jumped up and looked in the direction where Cody was waving at. He didn't move from his spot, but I could tell by the way he was acting, he also saw something. Jake noticed how Atlas was acting but didn't say anything and kept fishing. I didn't get too excited about it because Jake didn't. I wanted to enjoy the day with my family at the river. I was happy that Jake was with us that day.

# CHAPTER 2

## Summer 1979

Summer days are the longest; they're very hot and humid. Our farm was growing, and we were getting eggs from our chickens. We have also added a horse to our farm animals. Everyday Cody would have to see the horse and feed him. He named the horse Max.

Since getting our dog Atlas, I feel comfortable going out and exploring our property without feeling paranoid or a little uptight. I had planted tomatoes, cucumbers, squash, onions, and grapes in our little garden. The plants were growing well but not getting too many vegetables off them.

I have a schedule for my days with the children during the weekdays. It's so much different out here on the farm than it was in the city. In the city, I could go shopping, visit friends, and take the children to the park close to the schools where there are many children for Cody and Emma to play with. Here at the farm, it's chores, walking down the driveway to the mailbox, playing in the front yard or feeding the animals. I still loved our farm but, since Jake was still working at his job in the city, I was getting a little lonely during the weekdays. That's why I loved the weekends when Jake was off from work. After what he needs to do for the animals and his chores, he always found time to be with us and take us on adventures.

One sunny weekend, after Jake had finished attending to the animals and plowing the far end of the property for growing wheat, he came to the kitchen where I was finishing up with the morning dishes.

"Let's go to the river and go swimming." He said as he wrapped his arms around me and gave me a kiss.

I folded the dishtowel and went to get the children.

We headed to the back yard to the path that goes to the river. The path still looked like something that was being used always, but the children and I have not been on it since Jake told us not to go to the river without him. Although Jake has been to the river a few times to check the place out, the path was very much worn.

We arrived at the river and it was gently flowing now that the thunderstorms have passed and it's been dry for a few weeks. We walked over to the little sandy beach, and I spread a blanket on the sand for us all to sit on. Cody doesn't want to go into the water just yet; he wants to throw a few pebbles into the water. Jake took him over to where they found a few rocks to throw in.

I got up and went to the river to see how cold the water was. To my surprise, the water wasn't very cold at all. I could see the bottom of the river. I got into the river started wading out to the center of the river. I got about halfway to the center, and the water was just above my waist.

I was starting to enjoy the water and ducked down, so the water was up to my chin when suddenly, a huge rock was thrown right beside my head! I stood up quickly and turned around to look to see where Jake and the children were.

Jake was holding Emma and was standing near Cody where he was throwing the small pebbles at. They were looking at me. I was in the middle of the river asking Jake why he threw a rock at me when "SPLASH" came another rock on the other side of me. We all started looking around to see who was throwing the rocks!

I start wading back out of the water to the beach while Jake and Cody started making their way to the same place. Jake was still looking around to see if he could see anyone when another rock was thrown. I was getting a little frightened by this time. Jake yells out "HEY" so loud that we all were very startled.

We all were standing on the sandy beach when we heard a "whoop" coming from the other side of the river. Then as in sync, we heard another "whoop." This time it was behind us. Very close to the path that we must walk on to get back to our house.

By now, I became very frightened. I looked at Jake, and the look on his face was concerned. He looked frightened also. I was ready to go home at this point.

We started leaving the beach area with Jake leading the way carrying Emma and our small bag we brought out with us. I picked Cody up and carried him so we could walk faster. As soon as we started walking on the worn path back to the house, that same putrid smell hit us in the face. My heart started beating faster, and we started walking faster. When we got a little way down the path, we suddenly heard “whoop, whoop” coming from the other side of the river. This time it was louder than the last. It echoed throughout the woods. Thankfully, we didn’t hear the second one, unlike the first time. We walked as fast as we could back to the house.

When we came out of the woods, we could see the hog pen.

Something wasn’t right. The hog pen has been destroyed! I took the children inside the house while Jake went out to check on the hogs. He later came in and said that the hogs were huddled in a corner acting really scared. And one hog is missing, all except his head.

Now, who or what can rip a hog’s head off?

“I don’t know what could have done that,” Jake said as he sat down at the kitchen table, rubbing his forehead and sounding a little worried.

“I don’t know of any animal that can do that, not even a bear. What I do know is that I must get to the bottom of this, so I know if it’s safe for you and the kids to stay here alone while I go to work. I need to go talk to John".

That's what concerned me. Knowing that Jake will be leaving every morning to the city for work while the kids and I will be here alone with something that can rip a hog's head off.

That night after I put the children down to sleep, Jake was asleep when I came into the bedroom. I turned off the lamp beside the bed and laid down to sleep.

The night was warmer than I thought it would be. I got up out of bed to open the window in our bedroom. As I was laying back down on the bed, I heard a weird howling noise. A noise I have never heard before. It sounded like a low growl at first and rose to a long wail, back down to a guttural growl at the end. It wasn't too far off into the back woods, and it echoed throughout the night.

That scream sent a chill down my spine, and I was thinking of waking Jake to see if he knew what kind of animal that could make this sort of noise. Jake was in a deep sleep, so I let him be while I laid there listening to more screams.

I thought that might have been a onetime scream when, suddenly, I heard another scream! This time it sounded closer to the house. My body stiffened, and I could not move. I didn't know what to do after that noise that came through the opened window.

I was so focused on listening to the sounds coming from outside; that I did not notice the rustling going on inside the house. Emma had woke up. She was moving in her crib when she suddenly started crying. That made me forget about the noise from outside. I got out of bed and went into her bedroom. She was sitting up in her crib looking toward her open bedroom window.

I went to Emma and picked her up, and she started pointing to the window and still crying. I tried to comfort her, and she calmed down and put her head on my shoulder.

"What's wrong Emma? I asked her.

She lifted her head and pointed to the window. I was a bit afraid to look out the window because I might see something I didn't want to see.

I went to the window with Emma, and we looked out for the yard and surrounding area.

"There is nothing out there to be afraid of," I said to Emma.

Emma looked out the window, and I showed her the street light that Jake put up recently in the barn, it lights up the whole side of the yard so we can see every area of the yard.

Emma relaxed in my arms and was ready to go back to sleep. I put her in the crib and went back to my room and climbed into my bed.

The next day I got up very early in the morning and fixed breakfast for Jake and saw him off to work. I went out to the clothes line to hang the laundry up to dry. I noticed that the grass was getting tall and I was afraid that snakes would be attracted to the tall grass.

"It's time to mow," I said to myself.

I went to the barn and pulled the old mower out of its parking space and checked to see if it had any gas. It did, and I was ready to push it to the front of the house and start on the front lawn first.

I proceeded to the front of the house where I planted some flowers close to the front porch and stopped in my tracks.

Most of my flowers were laying on the ground trampled down in the dirt! But that was not what startled me the most. There was a huge footprint there. The size I have never seen before! And the print has toes! A bare footprint! Who could have done this? Then I remember the footprint that I found by the clothes line when we first came here. It looked identical to that one.

I started looking at the surrounding area and towards the woods. I was still in a bit of shock, so I just left the lawn mower on the front porch and headed into the house and waited for Jake to come back from work.

It was a long wait for him to come home, and as soon as he came through the front door, I stopped him in a somewhat panic mode trying to tell him about what I have discovered.

"Whoa, hold on a minute," Jake said in a concerned voice.

"Slow down a little so that I can understand you, darling."

I stopped talking and tried to catch my breath. Jake put his hands on my shoulders and led me to the sofa to sit down. I finally calmed down a little and told him to follow me.

He followed me down the front porch steps and to the flower garden. I pointed to the footprint in the soft dirt and the trampled flowers.

"What the hell?" Jake said in a low tone. He knew the kids were there on the porch right behind him and didn't want to scare them more than what I did in my panic mode.

"What kind of animal can do this?" I asked Jake as if he has all the right answers that I want to hear.

Jake ran his fingers through his thick curly hair and said,

"I don't have a clue, but if someone is trying to play a joke on us, I'm not happy with it, and I will get to the bottom of it."

Jake turned and started going back to the front porch, and he bends down to pick Emma up and swung her around his arms and ruffles Cody's hair and asked them how their day has been.

I followed him up to the front door and turned to look back through the woods thinking there must be a good explanation for all this.

A couple of weeks had gone by and the days were getting hotter and more humid as the summer drags on. It's a Saturday, and we have invited our neighbors John and Karen out to our house for a cookout and a much-needed social visit.

We were having a very enjoyable time talking, playing with the children, with chicken and hamburgers on the grill, and laughing.

Jake and John was by the grill talking about farming while Karen and I were watching the kids. It was getting to be about dusk, and the fireflies were coming out, and the children were chasing them around the yard trying to catch them.

Karen was in the middle of telling me about her beautiful roses blooming and lining her driveway when suddenly, she stops mid-sentence and started staring at the woods.

"What is that? Karen asked, wide-eyed and close to the edge of her chair, pointing at the tree line close to the barn.

"What is what? I asked her, turning in the direction to where she was pointing at.

"That!" she said.

At that time, Jake and John were listening to Karen, and they also focused their face to where she was pointing at. It wasn't very hard to see what she was pointing at.

Two glowing red round eyes were looking our way from the woods! The red eyes were swaying slowly from side to side, then suddenly they disappeared!

"Jada, take the kids inside the house and stay there," Jake said as he and John started walking down the barn toward where the glowing red eyes were.

I jumped up and grabbed Cody while Karen picked Emma up, and we head to the house.

About 30 minutes later, we heard Jake and John coming through the back door in the kitchen. They were carrying the food we left out on the grill and tables in the side yard.

"What did you find?" I asked Jake

"Nothing out of the way" Jake responded.

"We couldn't find anything, it must have been some kind of reflection," John said as he puts the food on the kitchen table. "It was very strange though," he said as we all sat down at the table to finish what we started from outside.

It was getting late in the night when we finished our dinner and social gathering in the front living room. The children were put to bed when John and Karen were ready to leave. Jake walked John and Karen to their car, and we all said goodnight and Jake and I watched them drive down our long driveway.

We both went into the house and straight to our bedroom for some much-needed rest. We were exhausted. Jake fell asleep almost immediately after laying down. I put my sleepwear on, laid down and fell into a deep sleep.

It seemed as no time had passed when I heard Cody up and playing with his toys in his room. I opened my eyes, and it was daylight. It was eight o'clock in the morning. Time to get up.

I got up and went downstairs to the kitchen to cook breakfast. While I was getting the frying pan out and putting it on the stove, I heard Cody following me to the kitchen and wanted a glass of orange juice. I gave him a small glass and set him down at the kitchen table. I went over to the window and opened the curtains for some much-needed light. As I was opening the curtains, I noticed mud was smeared on the window. As I kept looking at the smeared mud, it started to look like a huge handprint.

"It can't be a handprint! That is too big to be a handprint" I thought to myself.

I kept staring at the smeared mud print on the window, and I didn't notice Jake coming into the kitchen.

He wrapped his arms around me, and I jumped, as he held me tighter.

"What are you looking at?" Jake asked as he also found the mud smear.

I didn't have to say anything because he let go of me and went out the back door. He came to the window from outside looking at the smear and the ground as if he was looking for other things that are not supposed to be there.

As Jake was looking at the surrounding area around the house, he turned and looked at the barn and went towards the hog pen. I lost sight of him, and I finished up cooking breakfast.

Jake came in through the kitchen door and sat down to eat his breakfast. He was quiet and looked as if something was bothering him. I didn't want to interrupt his breakfast, but I was curious of what was bothering him.

"Anything wrong with the barn?" I asked in a low tone.

"Yeah," Jake said as he finishes his last bite of breakfast.

"The barn's back door was pried open, and the horse is acting a little weird, very skittish, the hogs are all huddled in the corner of the pen, and one hog is missing. I'm going to see if I can find it." Jake said.

Jake got up from the table and went to the phone that is in the front living room, while I fed the children and cleaned the dishes off the table.

After about five minutes later, Jake came back into the kitchen and told me that John is coming over with his horse and the two of them are riding back to the end of our property to try and find the hog.

It didn't take long before John showed up in the driveway with his horse trailer attached to his truck. Jake walked out through the front door to greet him. I can hear them discussing the weird things going on around our property. John has a concerned look on his face, and I wonder what he knew that he was not telling us. John and Karen have been living in this area for a very long time. If they know of anyone messing around with other people's property, they would know who they are, and I hope they can do something about it so the kids and I can enjoy our time outside in our yard without being afraid.

As I watched Jake and John riding their horses down to the tree line at the back of the property, I saw Atlas in front of them with his nose to the ground. I silently said a prayer for their safe return and maybe, just maybe, have a good explanation of what is going on around here.

About four o'clock that evening, I watched Jake and John rode their horses up to the barn and put our horse back into the stable for the day. I went out to meet them as they were putting John's horse back into the trailer.

"Did you find anything?" I asked

"Didn't find a damn thing," John said as he wipes sweat from his forehead with a handkerchief.

"What's strange is how the hog got out of the pen with no tracks to follow? "

I didn't have an answer to John's question.

"Where is Atlas?" I asked, looking around to see if I can see him.

"We don't know. He took off into the woods, and we have been looking for him to return and he never did. Maybe he will be back later this evening" Jake said as he shuts the door of the horse trailer.

John started his truck and heads down the driveway as we watched him disappear in the thick woods of our front yard.

Another month went by without any odd occurrences happening around our property, and I started getting comfortable going out in the yard with the children once again. Sadly though, Atlas has not returned home, and I began to think that we will never see him again.

# CHAPTER 3

## Autumn 1979

The summer was hot, but it's a come to an end and autumn has begun with the winds picking up and cooling everything down. Autumn is my favorite season of the year. Leaves were turning orange, yellow, and red colors, making the mountain look so beautiful.

The last month of summer had been very dry with hardly any rain in the whole month, making the farm and our garden hard to be watered.

Jake was still working at his job in the city, but we were getting closer to our farm being profitable enough for him to quit his job. With the wheat planted and getting more farm animals to raise as food, the chickens laying their eggs, getting the field plowed up for a large amount of corn to be planted; I guessed it would take a couple of years before he'll be able to quit and be at home with us full time.

One morning after Jake left for work, I went out on the front porch and was in awe of how beautiful the day was. The wind was blowing very cool, and the sun shining on my face felt so wonderful. The ground was very dry, and my curiosity got the best of me. I wanted to go down to the river to see what it would look like now since the dry spell.

"It wouldn't take long to walk to the river and come back," I thought to myself.

I went back to the house and prepared the children, and we went through the kitchen to the back door. We took the path that we haven't been on in a long time.

I felt so pleased to be out in the woods once again and didn't think of anything else but to get to the river and enjoy a little bit of the cool day. I didn't take anything along because we were not going to stay long.

When we arrived at the river, I was surprised at how low the water was. The dry spell we had last month had really made the water level very low. The river was so low that I could walk almost to the middle of the river. Just a small stream was flowing now.

As I was looking at the slow-moving stream in the middle of the river, Cody was by the big boulder that we would use the few times we came here. I walked over to where he was and stopped in my tracks, staring at the ground. Another huge footprint in the mud right where Cody was standing! I started looking around, and I started seeing more footprints. I looked to see where the prints were headed and I noticed a pattern. The prints were going to the stream in the middle of the river, and then back out into the woods.

I grabbed Cody up, (I still had Emma carrying her on my hip) and started running to the path. I began to pray to make it back home and at the same time cursing myself for coming here and putting my children in danger.

"How could I be so stupid" I kept telling myself repeatedly, running as fast as I could down the path toward the opening of the tree line.

As I was nearing the opening of the woods, my legs started shaking and getting weak. I was out of breath, and I had to slow down. All I could think of was to get out of the woods. I made it to the opening and stopped. I had to stop, or I would fall with two children that I was carrying.

I caught my breath and started walking toward the house. We finally made it to the back porch, and I sat down in the rocking chair by the door. I was still a little shaken by what I saw by the river, but now it seems not so frightening. All I could think of was that someone was playing a mean game around our woods. But how did they know I was going to go to the river to see them today? None of it made sense to me. And the next question was if I would tell Jake what I saw or not. He told me not to go into the woods when he isn't here, and he would be upset if I did tell him that I took our children back down to the river, alone, with no means of protection.

By the time Jake came home that evening, I had finished the laundry, and dinner was on the table. He looked very tired, and I didn't want to tell him about my adventure into the woods or get him upset. I decided I would tell him another time. Besides, I didn't want to hear him tell me again not to go to the woods. I had already made my own mind up that I would not go back into those woods without him.

That night as I was lying in bed thinking of the day's adventure, I began to get a chill. I noticed that the bedroom window was still open and the night air was getting cooler. I got out of my bed to close the window. As I got closer to the window to shut it, I heard a noise. It was the same yell or scream that I heard before in the summer. I could just barely hear it as I stood next to the window. I knew whatever it was, it wasn't close to the house. I closed the window and jumped back into bed. I was too tired to think about it. I needed some rest.

A few weeks had gone by, and Jake was busy harvesting the wheat that has been growing during spring and summer. I absolutely love this time of the year. I walked out of the house to the back lawn and watched as he gathered all his challenging work and put it in bales for sale. I kept thinking of the money we will be making and how much closer we are for Jake to quit his job in the city.

As I was watching Jake on his tractor, I looked over to where the path that goes down to the river, and I saw a huge tree shaking violently back and forth. I noticed there was no wind that could make the tree move like that. Not only that, but no other trees are shaking or even moving! What is making this specific tree to move like that? While my attention was on the tree, Cody came to sit on my lap. I picked him up, and I pointed to the tree,

"Big man, big man, doing that mommy," Cody said as he watched the tree shake.

"What are you talking about Cody?" I asked, getting a little nervous.

Cody laughed and jumped off my lap and went to the edge of the field where his daddy was plowing.

I watched him wave at Jake and started running towards the tractor. Jake stopped the tractor and picked Cody up and carried him in the tractor.

I turned my attention back to the tree that was moving earlier but now it's not moving anymore. Was it my imagination that the tree was moving? No, I knew it was moving! But how? I said to myself.

I stood up and started going to the house to see if Emma had woke up from her nap when another tree suddenly starts to shake wildly right in front of the other tree. This tree was closer to the tree line, and I looked at Jake and pointed to the tree.

I got his attention, and he looked to where I was pointing and then, he stopped the tractor. As soon as he looked at the tree, the top of the tree comes crashing down to the ground.

Jake put the tractor in drive mode and stopped in front of me, handing Cody down for me to take him.

"Take him to the house," Jake said as he runs to the tree line with his pistol drawn (Jake always had a pistol on him).

I took Cody to the house and ran upstairs to check on Emma. She was still asleep, so I ran back downstairs to the kitchen window to watch for Jake to come out of the woods.

After about fifteen minutes, Jake came out of the woods walking toward his tractor. He starts it up and drove it down to the barn to park it for the day.

When Jake came into the kitchen, I started asking questions.

"What did you find? What was making the trees shake? Did you see anything?"

"Now calm down, I didn't find anything, and nothing was around those trees," Jake said as he sat down at the table.

"There's no explanation for what made the trees to shake like that. My guess would be maybe a bear was scratching his back on the trees."

"A bear? We have bears that close to the house?" I asked in a fearful tone.

"That's my only guess," Jake said as he looked at the ceiling, hearing Emma crying in her crib.

I turned around and went upstairs to attend to Emma, and I brought her down with the rest of us to the kitchen.

After hearing about bears in the woods, I got an uneasy feeling knowing full well that I do take our babies out in those woods where bears roam and could have easily run up on one. Now, thinking of bears, it makes perfect sense of all the footprints we have seen around our property. But what about the prints around the house? Do bears get that close to houses? I guess they do.

After being wary of staying at the farm when Jake goes to work, Jake assured me that bears would not bother the kids and me.

“It’s getting cold and bears hibernate during the winter,” Jake told me with a smirk on his face.

That made me feel a little better, and I could hardly wait till winter comes.

“As a matter of fact, they are probably bedding down now. Brown bears around here are scared of humans just as we are scared of them. Don’t let that bother you, Jada.” Jake said as he wraps his arms around me to comfort me.

“That does make me feel better about being here alone,” I said embracing his hug.

That night as I was getting ready for bed, I heard Cody in his room playing and talking to himself. I got up and went to his room. I opened his door, and he was by the window looking out toward the barn. I went over to the window and looked out to see what has his attention.

I looked out toward the barn, and I saw a shadow walking toward the barn and the hog pen. I started to hear the hogs moving around and grunting like they were getting spooked by something.

"A BEAR!" I said aloud as I turned and ran to our bedroom to wake Jake up and tell him that a bear is after the hogs.

Jake jumped up and grabbed a shotgun that sits by the side of the bed and moved downstairs with a flashlight to protect the hogs in the pen.

After about a minute had gone by, I heard the shotgun go off. Then I heard another shot ringed through the woods. I thought that Jake must have shot the bear and I won't have to worry about going outside with the kids during the day anymore.

Jake came back in and put the shotgun by the front door, sat down in his rocker chair and sighs.

"Are you sure you saw a bear?" Jake said as he looked at me.

"I saw something out there. I don't know if it was a bear, but it was big and walking toward the barn." I said as I sat down on the sofa.

"What I was shooting at was very big and looked to be walking a long way on two legs. I know bears can walk on their back legs for a brief period, but when I shot at it, it took off running through the woods breaking everything in its path." Jake said with a very shocked look on his face.

"If it wasn't a bear, then what was it?" I asked, not knowing what answer Jake would give me.

"I don't know, but it's gone now, and we need to go back to bed."

Jake got up from his rocker and headed up the stairs. I followed him as close as I could. I didn't want to be downstairs by myself, especially tonight.

The next morning Jake went out to the barn for his daily chores with the animals. I watched him as he carried the feed and water to the hogs and went to the barn to attend to Max.

After about five minutes later, I saw Jake opening the barn doors and lead Max out with his saddle on him. I moved outside through the back door to see what he was up to.

"I'm going to take Max for a ride down the trail to the woods to get him a little exercise. I'll be back within an hour", he said as he pulled up into the saddle.

I waved to him as he rode toward the back of the property, then I turned around and went back to the kitchen to start preparing for lunch.

About an hour went by and true to his words, I saw Jake coming back with Max from the woods. He went inside the barn and put Max back in his stable for him to eat and rest. Jake came out of the barn and went up to the back porch to sit in the rocker to pull his muddy boots off before coming into the house.

"How was your ride?" I asked as I sat down in the swing next to his rocker.

"Good," Jake said, being a man of few words.

"Great, and lunch is ready," I said still sitting in the swing, knowing there was more to Jake's story than what he was saying.

I didn't say anything else when Jake leaned his back on the rocker chair.

"I found a cave about a mile out in the woods, by the river upstream. It must be where an animal feeds because there were a bunch of animal bones piled up in it. Looked to be deer bones."

"Could it be a bear's den?" I asked, looking at him to see his body language and his expression on his face.

"It could be, all I know is that Max was really spooked when we got closer and wanted to run away from the cave." He said and then looked at me, "

"I also found Atlas."

I looked at Jake and knew that our Atlas was never coming back.

“I found his head in the cave with the other bones. I couldn’t find his body”. Jake said as he gets up to sit next to me and puts his arm around my shoulder.

“That’s just terrible,” I said as I laid my head on his shoulder, “I’m going to miss Atlas, but what are we going to do about the bear?”

“I’ll figure something out. Let’s go eat lunch before it gets cold.”

We both got up and went into the kitchen, Jake sat down at the table while I get the children and washed them up for lunch.

After lunch, Jake and I gathered the children up and head into town to go shopping for much-needed groceries and other necessities. It’s so nice to get away from the farm for a little while and enjoy the sights of the city. Jake also gave the children and me a fancy dinner at a new restaurant that was recently opened.

We all were having a very enjoyable time but it was getting late, and we needed to go back to the farm to feed the animals and put the groceries away.

Jake pulled the truck up to the front porch steps so it would be easier to unload the purchases and get them into the house before it gets dark.

As Jake went to the barn to feed the hogs and Max, I started unloading the bags from the bed of the truck. It was just getting dusk when I turned around with a load of bags in my hands, and something caught my eye right beside the hog pen. I could see in the woods right inside the tree line, two round, red glowing balls.  I stopped what I was doing and just stared at them.

As I was staring at them, they started moving from side to side. That frightened me. I couldn't see anything else but the glowing balls.

I wanted to yell at Jake because he was in the barn, but somehow, I could not move! It was as if I was paralyzed! I was getting more frightened by each second and tried to move and warn Jake of what I was looking at.

What seemed as time went by so slowly, I heard Emma crying out to me, and I came out of the trance I was in and back to reality. I ran up the front porch steps and put the groceries on the living room floor and ran back to yell at Jake. By the time I was running back down the steps, Jake was walking back to the house, and the glowing red balls in the woods were gone.

I ran to Jake pointing into the woods and trying to tell him what I saw as he was looking at me like I was losing my mind. He turned around to see what it was and suddenly, they were there again. I started panicking, and Jake took my arm, and we ran up the stairs and into the house. He grabbed his shotgun that was hanging on the wall in the living room and ran back through the front door. I grabbed the children, and we sat down on the sofa, waiting for Jake to come back in.

Jake came back into the house, and I could tell he was very frustrated. I didn't want to pressure him as to what he thought was going on around here, but I needed to know for my own sanity. But before I could ask him anything, he walked toward the phone and dialed the number to our neighbor John.

"Can you come over tomorrow? Jake asks John, who is on the other end of the phone line.

"Thanks, I'll see you in the morning," Jake said as he hangs the phone back on the base.

Jake got up and heads to the staircase and climbed to the second floor.

I took Cody and Emma, and we followed him, then, I put the children to bed. I made sure that their windows were closed and locked. Of course, we are on the second floor of the house and making sure the windows were locked seemed useless; it did make me feel that the children were safe and secure.

I went to our bedroom and Jake is already lying in bed. I got ready for bed and crawled under the covers beside him. He gave me a kiss and said goodnight while leaving me with so many questions to ask. Knowing Jake well, I know not to push it, and I turned off the lamp and tried to get some sleep.

I was awake the next morning to see that Jake was already out of bed and not a sound in the house. I jumped out of bed and ran to see if Cody and Emma were awake.

Surprisingly, both were still asleep. I closed both bedroom doors and headed downstairs. I came to the front door to see John's truck parked in front of the house.

I realized that both Jake and John had left the property and I will have to wait for them to come back and see if I could get any answers from them.

I went to the kitchen to prepare a cup of coffee for myself, and I sat down at the kitchen table to have a few minutes relaxation before the children would wake up and ask for their breakfast.

It was getting late in the evening when Jake and John came walking up from the back of the house to the back porch. The look on both of their faces got my attention. I also noticed that John was limping badly. He had injured his leg. I ran to the back porch to see if I could help them when John fell to the ground next to the back porch. Jake ran into the house and called Karen to come over.

I knelt down in front of John to see his injured leg. I raised the trouser on his leg to his knee and saw he has a big gash on his shin. I rushed to the kitchen for the first aid kit, (a do-it-yourself first aid kit is all we had at the time) and rushed back to his side. I started bandaging his leg and noticed his hands were shaking. I didn't want to pressure him with questions so I kept working on his leg to bandage it up so he can walk.

Not long, Karen was walking out of the kitchen down toward John and me with a worried look on her face. She bends down and kissed John on the forehead and told him that he needs to be more careful in the woods.

"You are not as young as you used to be and trampling in the woods is not for old people," she said with a smile on her face.

We helped John up off the ground, and he said his leg feels much better and we helped him to Karen's car.

"We will be back tomorrow to get John's truck, and don't worry about John; he will be okay," Karen said as she walks around to the driver's side of the car.

We waved to them as they head down the long driveway.

I turned to go back to the front porch and went into the house. I shut and lock the bolt on the door. Jake was sitting on the sofa with Cody and Emma on his lap. He was showing them something he found in the woods that day. Jake was showing them little arrow heads made from Native American Cherokee that lived in this area many years ago. Cody was very interested in it, and Emma was just happy to be sitting on her daddy's lap.

I went to the kitchen and prepared a cup of coffee for Jake and brought it to him. He dropped the kids down on the floor and took the coffee.

"There's dinner on the stove if you are hungry," I said as I sat next to him.

“I’ll eat in a few minutes,” Jake said as he sipped his coffee.

He took a few sips and looked down at the children playing on the floor and sighs.

“If I ever find out who is causing all this trouble around here, I probably will not call the police. I will take care of them myself,” Jake said as he kept staring at the floor.

“So, you think it is other people that are trying to scare us?” I asked.

“John said that a family that has been causing trouble around here for years have been wanting this property for a long time but couldn’t afford it. John thinks they are trying to scare us off so they can move in without paying for it.

“That’s not what I wanted to hear, that made me very nervous,” I said as I moved closer to Jake.

“John said he would pay them a visit and get everything taken care of.”

“I really hope so, and I will be very scared to be here alone when you go back to work.”

“I’m taking two weeks off for a vacation to get some things done around here”. Jake said as he got up and went to the kitchen to eat his dinner.

“Thank God,” I said with a sigh and followed him into the kitchen to fix a plate of food for him.

A week later Karen called to tell us that the family that wanted our property have moved away, and no one knows where they went to, and she also told us that John was healing very well from his leg injury. That was a relief for me to know that we don't have to deal with them and maybe everything will get back to normal around here.

"That's great to hear, Karen," I told her as I opened the front door and saw what a beautiful day it was. "Thank you for calling, and I am so glad that John's leg is getting better."

I put the phone back on the base and took Cody and Emma up and took them outside to enjoy the beautiful day. I felt so relieved that I don't have to worry about other people coming to the house to do harm to my family especially when Jake was not around.

But, I couldn't let the fear of the things around here hinder me on getting things done to prepare for winter. I watched Cody and Emma play in the back yard as I gathered all the vegetables that I could, out of our little garden and tried canning them for winter. As I was gathering the vegetables in the garden, I could hear Jake chopping firewood for the fireplace to warm the house when the cold comes.

Amazingly, we did so much work around the property, and both Jake and I were exhausted but happy with how everything was working so smoothly. With a stockpile of firewood, and our cellar full of groceries for winter, we had a little time to relax in the evenings and watch the children play in the backyard.

As we were sitting on the back porch, enjoying the evening and watching the kids play, we heard someone driving up our driveway toward the house. Jake got up to see who was visiting us and walked beside the house toward the front to meet them.

It was a car that we didn't know, and as the car stopped, a man got out from the car and introduced himself as Bill. He clearly looked upset. I walk toward the front of the house the same way Jake did and watched as Jake and Bill discussed. Bill kept looking back toward the road and pointing in the same direction as if he was explaining something to Jake. Both were talking in a muffled voice, and I couldn't hear what was being said. Jake kept listening to him and nodding his head, and then they shook hands, Bill got back into his car and Jake walked back toward the side of the house. We both walked back to the backyard to watch the kids.

"Who was that?" I asked.

"That was Bill. He lives with his wife down the road about three miles from here. He said that there have been weird things going on around his house and have seen an unidentified animal walking beside the main road at night. He wanted to let us know that it was close to our property that he saw it walking." Jake said as he sat down on the steps of the back porch.

"And he couldn't identify the animal? What does that mean? I asked as if Jake has all the answers.

"I don't know but the countryside has many wild animals, and we have protection. How do we know if Bill isn't crazy himself? Don't let it bother you."

It did bother me.  And I knew it was getting closer to the time for Jake to go back to the city for his job.

Another week had gone by, and Jake have to gone back to work on Monday. We have had a great two weeks with him being at home with the kids and me, and everything was working just fine on the farm. No incidents have occurred, and everyone is comfortable and happy. I did have some anxiety about how the days will be when Jake is not here. Will I feel safe then?

# CHAPTER 4

## Winter 1979

Winter weather was finally here, and the house was feeling very warm and cozy. Surprisingly, the old farm house was much insulated and stayed warm throughout the whole winter.

The first snow storm came on the same day as Cody's fourth birthday. I had baked a cake for the very important day, and Cody was very excited to be a year older.

Jake and I wanted the day to be calm and sunny so we could wrap the children up and go outside in the yard so that Cody could play with his birthday presents. But the storm was getting worse, and the wind was howling and blowing snow everywhere as it was snowing very heavily. We had to stay indoors, and Cody had to wait until the weather gets better to play with his outdoor toys.

The good news about the storm was that Jake was snowed in and couldn't make it down the mountain into town for work. He kept the fireplace full of the firewood that he stocked piled near the front porch, and we settled in for a peaceful night and huddled together listening to the raging snow storm outside.

I made homemade vegetable beef soup with the vegetables that I had canned earlier in the year, with homemade cornbread. To us, that was a fancy feast, and everyone was enjoying the night in our warm house.

About eight o'clock that night, while the storm was still raging, Jake had to go check on the farm animals and to make sure they were safe in the storm. After a while, he came back inside and said the animals were safe and sound. That's a relief, for I had never seen a snow storm this bad before. I was thinking of all the wild animals and wondering how they all stay safe in storms like this. I guessed that God gave them common sense to get out of the weather. It is known that animals know when something about the weather or earthquakes are about to happen so I thought they would know about the snow storm was going to happen before we did.

It was getting late, and it was time to give the children their baths and put them to bed. The storm was letting up, and the wind stopped blowing so hard. I put Cody and Emma to bed and went downstairs to the front living room where Jake was sitting in his rocker reading a book.

I sat down on the sofa and picked up a book that I have been reading for a while now. I flip through the pages to find where I stopped the last time I was reading the book when, suddenly, Jake and I heard something hit the side of the house.

Jake looked up from his book, but he sat there for a minute. As soon as he looked down at his book, something hits the side of the house again.

This time Jake dropped his book and got up from his rocker, went to the kitchen window and looked out to see if he could see anything.

The storm was moving away and it had stopped snowing. The wind was calm and there were about ten inches of snow on the ground. Jake opened the back door to the porch to see what was hitting the house. As he was looking out the back door, something hit the house closer to the front door.

Jake closed the back door and walked to where his boots and coat were kept.

He grabbed his shotgun that was hanging on the wall by the front door and stepped out onto the front porch.

"I'll be back in a minute. I need to see what is hitting the house" Jake said as he closes the front door.

"Hurry back," I said as I watched him go out.

Soon, Jake was back in the house with a huge rock in his hand.

"Where did you find that?" I asked, looking at the rock he had in his hand.

"That is what hit the house" Jake said as he dropped the rock by the fireplace.

"There's another rock out there that is bigger than this one. That's the second one that hit the house."

“But who could be out there throwing rocks at the house?” I asked,

“And why?”

“I don’t know darling,” Jake said as he sat down on his rocker.

“I didn’t see anything, but these rocks and the animals are all safe. I’ll look around tomorrow to see if I can find anything.”

With that, Jake said it was time for bed. I checked on the front and back doors to make sure they were locked and secured before heading upstairs for the night.

The next morning was bright and sunny, and I was glad that the storm was over. Jake was up before me, and I figured he was out checking on the animals to be sure they were doing well after the storm.

I checked on Cody and Emma to see if they were awake yet, then I went downstairs and straight to the kitchen to prepare breakfast for Jake and the children. I prepared a cup of coffee and pulled the curtains back from the windows.

I look out the window to see if I could find Jake anywhere, but as I started looking at the snow, I saw footprints in the snow.

Thinking the footprints may be Jake’s prints, I follow the footprints, and I realize that they came close to the house. As I followed them, they came up to the back porch and up the steps.

I went to the back door and opened it and made a startling discovery. Right there at the back door, on the back porch, was huge footprints! Huge, Bare footprints!

Those are not Jake's boot prints! And they don't look like a bear's footprints either!

Startled, I closed the door as fast as I could, put on my coat, and ran out the front door towards the barn where Jake was feeding the horse. As I was running to the barn, I saw Jake's boot prints and follow them. They were not as big as the footprints on the back porch.

As I reached the barn door, Jake was just coming out and met me in the doorway.

"What are you doing out here in this mess darling?" Jake asked in a surprised tone.

"You have to come look at this," I said, gasping for air.

"Whoa, what is it?" Jake asked grabbing my arm to calm me down.

"On the back porch, there're footprints!" I said trying to catch my breath to tell him.

He let go of my arm and started walking toward the back porch. He didn't walk far before he stopped and saw the footprints in the yard going to the back of the house.

“Get in the house!” he said as he pulled his handgun from the holster on his hip.

I tried running in the snow. It was slow going, but I made it to the front door and shut it behind me. I ran to the kitchen and to the back door where Jake was standing looking around and studying the footprints. I opened the back door, and he walked in.

“Looks like those troublemakers are back,” Jake said as he walked to the sink to get a glass of water.

“The neighbors that want this property?” I asked.

“Yes, I’m afraid so, sweetheart.” But don’t worry, I’ll take care of it.” Jake said as he walked to the front door to start his truck.

I watched as Jake went to the truck and started it up to warm the inside so we could put the children in so they will not get cold. He walked back to the house and told me to get the children bundled up, that we were going to John and Karen’s house to pay them a visit and talk to them about what could be done about the neighbors that were giving us so much trouble.

“That doesn’t sound good,” John said as he listened to Jake and what we have been experiencing around our property.

“I met the sheriff in town; he said that those neighbors are gone. They just disappeared! That is what he said. John said as he rubbed his forehead as to be thinking and not knowing what to do.

“Not just disappeared, but they left everything they owned, even their truck is parked in front of the house. Like the Sheriff said, they just disappeared.”

“That’s strange.” Replied Jake.

“Yes, it is. If you want to go up there to see for yourself, I will go up there with you. We will get to the bottom of this.” John said as he waits for Jake to reply.

“Let’s go,” Jake said as he slowly gets up from his chair and looked at me.

Jake told me that I would be safe with Karen while he and John go up to the troublesome neighbor’s house to have a look around. I hope they don’t run into any problems and come back safe and soon.

After some time while Jake and John were gone, Karen tries to stay calm and keeps telling me that everything will be back to normal after the men come back with some information for us. I wanted to believe her and would just nod in agreement as she told me over and over that Jake will be safe.

We put the children down for a nap when we finally saw the headlights from John’s truck coming down the driveway. We waited patiently for the men to come in through the doorway before the questions that were bundled up inside us started flying out of our mouths.

“Did you find anything? Were they there? What happened?” Is everything okay? These were the questions that flew out of my mouth and Karen’s mouth.

"Whoa, slow down!" Jake said as I was holding on to his arm as if he would walk away without answering our questions.

"Yes, we did find that the property was abandoned, but all their belongings are still there. The house was unlocked, so we went in to see if anyone was in there. No one was there, and everything was in its place." John said as he pulls his coat off and hangs it on the coat hanger by the front door.

"The weird thing was, the kitchen table had plates full of food on them like they were ready to eat their dinner. But the food was untouched, and the house was very cold. No fire or any kind of heat in the house." Jake said after John finished what he wanted to say. "Just like the Sheriff said, it looks as if they just disappeared."

I didn't know what to think about the information that the men have come back with. All I knew was that we didn't have to worry about the neighbors anymore, but now we must worry about what is lurking around our property.

I took the children and said goodnight to John and Karen as we went out through the front door to our truck. As we turn into our driveway, I couldn't help but wonder who or what was roaming around in these mountains and if it was safe to live here with our precious children.

I went to the kitchen to prepare dinner while Jake poked at the hot embers in the fireplace and puts more firewood in to keep the fire going. I went to the back door to make sure the door is locked. While checking to see if the door is locked, I got the courage to look out the window to see if there is anything that looked different. To my relief, I couldn't see anything. I simply went to where the stove was placed and started preparing dinner.

I prepared dinner with the left-over pot roast that we had the night before, with green beans that I canned earlier in the year that came out of our small garden. With that, we had mashed potatoes and corn bread. We all sat down at the kitchen table and enjoyed a very delicious meal, and I savored the family time that we haven't had in a long time.

A few weeks after that, the children were getting very excited about Christmas. I had decorated the farmhouse in Christmas lights, and Jake brought home a beautiful evergreen tree that was so big that the top almost touched the twelve-foot ceiling. We put the tree in front of the big picture window in the first living room. After it had been decorated with lights and ribbons, it was the most beautiful tree I had ever seen. The children were in awe with all the festive décor around the house. I decorated little trees in their rooms also, which doubled the lights in their room.

It was time to go into town to buy our necessities and a few Christmas gifts for Cody and Emma. Jake took the children into another part of the store as I snuck around the store to hide the gifts we were getting for them.

It was very exciting for all of us to be in town and shopping for Christmas. The town was festive with bright twinkling lights in all the windows of the stores and lining the roads, seeing the Christmas Carolers going around singing their songs, children sitting on Santa's lap and telling him what they wanted for Christmas. I had so much fun in town than the farmhouse with so many people around laughing and being with their families, enjoying the festive activities. I dreaded going back to the farmhouse in the woods and silently wished we were living in town once again.

Soon, we were heading out of town and going back to the mountains for home. When we pulled up to our old farmhouse, with the beautiful Christmas tree lit up and filling up the picture window, and the lights twinkling around the front porch, I forgot about the city and fell in love with the house again. This was home, and I felt at peace for the first time in a long time.

Jake and I carried the sleeping children out of the truck and took them upstairs to their rooms for the night. Then we unloaded the groceries and the presents that will be presented to the children on Christmas day.

When we had everything put up and hid, Jake and I were exhausted and headed up for bed.

Christmas day was very exciting. The children got up early in the morning to see what Santa Clause brought them on the night before Christmas. There were Christmas presents underneath the big tree. Cody and Emma could hardly wait to open them. Jake and I watched the children opened the presents with glee in their eyes. When all the presents were opened, the children sat and played with all the toys they received allowing me to go to the kitchen to prepare breakfast and put a fresh ham in the oven.

Jake went out to feed the animals and to pick up some eggs for me to cook for breakfast. In my mind, it seemed to be taking a long time for him to come back in and I started wondering if anything was wrong with the animals. I kept looking out the kitchen window toward the barn and the chicken coop to see if I could see what he was doing, but before I could see him coming to the house, the back door opened and Jake came in with a half dozen of eggs in his hands. I took the eggs from him and went to the sink to wash them before cracking them open to fry.

Not long after, breakfast was served, the aroma of the meal filled the house from top to bottom. I thought this would be the best Christmas we have had in a very long time.

Jake took the children outside to play in the snow that was still on the ground from the last snow fall, while I cleaned all the Christmas paper and toys that were left on the living room floor.

As I was cleaning the house, and Jake was outside with the children, a loud yell rang out from outside. The yell came from the back of the house. It was the same yell I would hear at night back in the summer months, but much, much louder. It sounded like it was just inside the tree line right behind our house!

I ran to the kitchen to look out the back door to see if I could find Jake and the children. As soon as I opened the back door, Jake came in through the front door carrying Cody and Emma. He shut the door and grabbed his shotgun.

"Lock the doors and don't come out no matter what happens," Jake said as he reaches out for the front door.

"What was that?" I asked while running to the front door to lock it as Jake walked out to the front porch.

"I don't know, but it is close to the barn. Stay inside the house!"

I closed the door and locked it just as Jake had ordered me to. I turned around to face the children as they were standing behind me looking at me with wide eyes and a puzzled look on their faces.

As soon as I looked at Cody, he started to shrug his shoulders and then told me something that made my blood run cold.

"That was the big man in the woods," Cody said.

"What are you talking about Cody, what big man?" I asked as I held him and sat on the sofa.

"The big man that comes to my window sometimes. He is nice and tries to talk to me." Cody said as he sat beside me on the sofa.

"Cody quit telling me stories, buddy," I said to him, studying his facial expressions to see if he was just saying that to get my attention.

"I'm not mommy, he came to my window, and I tried to talk to him, but he doesn't want to talk back," Cody said with a very serious look on his face.

I began to get frightened by what Cody was telling me. His bedroom window is on the second floor, and there is no way a man can come to his window and "try" to talk to Cody in the middle of the night.

As I was talking to Cody and trying to get more information about what he was talking about, Jake came in through the front door carrying his shotgun on his shoulder. I got up and asked him what was going on outside then I realized I had left something undone in the kitchen.

I went to the kitchen and removed the ham I initially placed in the oven. It was baked perfectly with a golden brown glaze covering it. I started thinking about what to prepare to go with the ham to have the best Christmas dinner when Jake came in and told me he would call John and the two of them will be going out into the woods to hunt for this animal that is making the “yells” and disturbing our farm animals.

John pulled up to the house and got out of his truck carrying a shotgun over his shoulder. Jake went out to meet him, and they both walked to the front porch and came into the front living room. I walked out of the kitchen to the room where they were talking and I listened to their conversation.

“We will find it this time.” I heard John telling Jake as they prepare to go out in the freezing weather with their weapons, hunting for an unknown animal in the woods.

As I was watching the men preparing to go hunting, I was very anxious to tell them what Cody told me earlier, but before I could get their attention, they were already opening the door and walking out on the porch.

I said a silent prayer for their safety and went back to the kitchen to finish the dinner I was preparing and hoped that the men would come home soon.

Time went by so slowly, and the men were not back from their hunting trip. Dinner was ready and getting cold; the children were fed, bathed, and ready for bed yet they were not back. It was very dark outside from the clouds hiding the moon and stars, and I kept wondering what the men were doing and how close are they from the house. The more time had passed, the more worried I became.

Suddenly, as if my prayers were answered, the front door was opened, and the men came in. I jumped up from the sofa and met them at the door. Jake was helping John walk into the house, and I noticed that John looked exhausted.

Jake helped John to the sofa and sits him down and tries to make him comfortable. Jake swiftly walked to the back door to make sure it was locked, came back into the living room and stood by the fireplace to warm his hands.

Neither of the men was talking, and they had a very concerned look on their faces. I was hesitant to ask them any questions about their hunting trip, but the suspense was killing me.

"Dinner is ready and getting cold; I'll go fix you two a plate," I said as I head towards the kitchen.

"I've got to be going," John said as he got up from the sofa and walked toward the front door.

"Are you okay to drive home?" Jake asked as he followed John to the door.

"Yes, I'm okay, just very tired and getting to old to be tramping into the woods," John replied, still with concerned expression in his eyes.

"Thank you for coming out and helping me," Jake said as he accompanied John to his truck.

Jake came back into the house and sat on his rocker chair. Then he got up and stood in front of the fireplace with his hands on the mantle and his head down staring into the fire.

"What did you find in the woods?" I asked slowly and in a lowered voice as if I really didn't want to know the truth.

Jake started shaking his head slowly back and forth still staring at the fire in the fireplace.

"It's almost unbelievable," Jake said as he kept staring at the fire.

"What do you mean by that?" I asked as I walked closer to him, wanting to know more than what he is saying.

Jake turned to me and put his hands on my shoulders, stared right into my eyes as if he sees right through to my soul.

"John and I ran up on a..."

"What?" I asked getting impatient and scared at the same time as I felt Jake's hands starting to shake while still holding my shoulders.

"A Bigfoot, Jada!" he said as he slowly let go of my shoulders and puts his hands back on the mantle.

I stood there by the fireplace trying to understand what Jake had told me and thinking I must have misunderstood what he had just said.

I kept staring at him as he kept staring at the fire in the fireplace as if his mind was a million miles away. My mind was going full speed trying to comprehend what was just said to me.

"What did you say?" I asked, standing still with my heart racing and pounding in my ears.

"But Bigfoot is not real," I said, not being able to move and still staring at Jake.

"I saw it, Jada, they are real."

## Conclusion

Being a city girl living out in the countryside can be very overwhelming of the different noises and sights that come from everyday living. I never thought of being in the woods living with bears, bobcats, snakes, and other wild animals. But I can get used to that. But when my husband came in and told me of another creature living in the woods close to our farmhouse, that was when I thought that living in the countryside may not be for my children and me. Especially a Bigfoot!

Be sure to read "Sharing the Mountain with Bigfoot, the second year."

Made in the USA
Middletown, DE
27 July 2021

44917545R00040